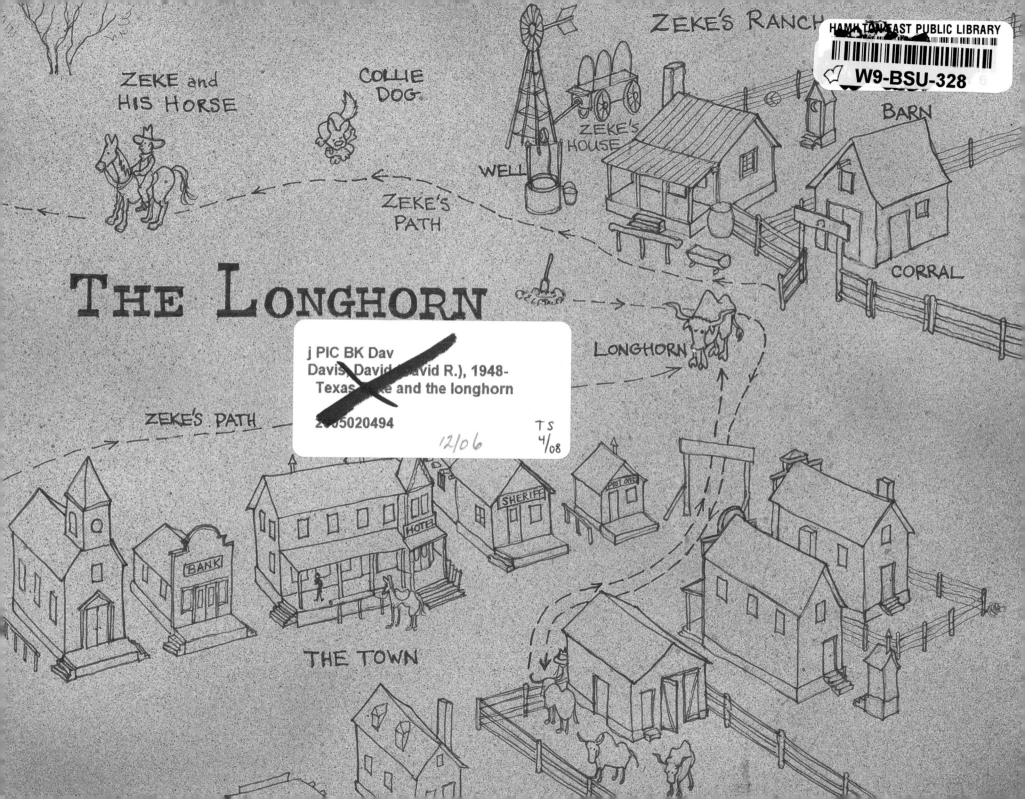

Texas Zeke and the Longhorn

Texas Zeke and the Longhorn

By David Davis
Illustrated by Alan Fearl Stacy

PELICAN PUBLISHING COMPANY
GRETNA 2006

*For my mother, Margie, my brother, Michael, and my sister, Jan. Also, for
Doc Calhoun, who gave me the chance to write stories, and for my editor,
Nina Kooij, and my assistant editor, Lindsey Reynolds. Finally, for Texas, the
magical, mythical land where I was raised. —DRD*

*For my mom, Jean, the original "pretty gal," who
loved horses and Texas. —AFS*

*The word "Pelican" and the depiction of a pelican are trademarks
of Pelican Publishing Company, Inc., and are registered in the
U.S. Patent and Trademark Office.*

Library of Congress Cataloging-in-Publication Data

Davis, David (David R.), 1948-
  Texas Zeke and the longhorn / by David Davis ; illustrated by Alan Fearl Stacy.
     p. cm.
  Summary: A cumulative tale set in Texas, in which a cowboy seeks help in herding his long-
horn steer into the corral.
  ISBN-13: 978-1-58980-348-0 (hardcover : alk. paper)
  [1. Folklore.] I. Stacy, Alan, ill. II. Title.
  PZ8.1.D2887Tex 2006
  398.2'09764'02—dc22

2005020494

Printed in China

Published by Pelican Publishing Company, Inc.
1000 Burmaster Street, Gretna, Louisiana 70053

TEXAS ZEKE AND THE LONGHORN

One morning an old Texas cowboy named Zeke found a Spanish gold piece while working at his ranch. "What can I do with this coin?" he asked.

"Why, I'll ride into town and buy a longhorn steer!
When I get home, I'll eat a big bowl of hot chili."

Zeke bought the longhorn, herded him home,
and opened the gate to the corral.

He pushed and pulled and tugged and shoved, but the steer wouldn't budge.

Zeke left the longhorn and rode for help. He met a border collie chewing on a bone. Zeke tipped his hat and said, "Collie, collie, herd the steer. Steer won't go in corral, and I won't get home for chili."
But the collie wouldn't herd the steer.

As Zeke walked his pony, he saw a mesquite stick waving in the wind. He tipped his hat and said, "Stick, stick, poke the collie. Collie won't herd steer; steer won't go in corral; and I won't get home for chili."

But the stick wouldn't poke the collie.

Traveling along the trail, Zeke saw beans cooking on a campfire. He tipped his hat and said, "Fire, fire, burn the stick. Stick won't poke collie; collie won't herd steer; steer won't go in corral; and I won't get home for chili."

But the fire wouldn't burn the stick.

Zeke moseyed along the trail and came upon a spring of water bubbling out of the ground. With a tip of his hat he said, "Water, water, quench the fire. Fire won't burn stick; stick won't poke collie; collie won't herd steer; steer won't go in corral; and I won't get home for chili."

But the water wouldn't quench the fire.

Zeke trotted his pony along and met a javelina digging acorns. He tipped his hat and said, "Javelina, javelina, drink the water. Water won't quench fire; fire won't burn stick; stick won't poke collie; collie won't herd steer; steer won't go in corral; and I won't get home for chili."

But the javelina wouldn't drink the water.

Zeke spotted a burro eating grass next to the trail. He tipped his hat and said, "Burro, burro, kick the javelina. Javelina won't drink water; water won't quench fire; fire won't burn stick; stick won't poke collie; collie won't herd steer; steer won't go in corral; and I won't get home for chili."

But the burro wouldn't kick the javelina.

Zeke spurred his pony along the trail and saw a prickly pear cactus growing in the sun. Tipping his hat, he said, "Cactus, cactus, jab the burro. Burro won't kick javelina; javelina won't drink water; water won't quench fire; fire won't burn stick; stick won't poke collie; collie won't herd steer; steer won't go in corral; and I won't get home for chili."

But the cactus wouldn't jab the burro.

Zeke rode farther. He saw an armadillo digging a hole. Zeke tipped his hat and said, "Armadillo, armadillo, dig the cactus. Cactus won't jab burro; burro won't kick javelina; javelina won't drink water; water won't quench fire; fire won't burn stick; stick won't poke collie; collie won't herd steer; steer won't go in corral; and I won't get home for chili."

But the armadillo wouldn't dig the cactus.

Zeke spied a young cowhand mooning over a pretty gal. He tipped his hat and said, "Cowhand, cowhand, chase the armadillo. Armadillo won't dig cactus; cactus won't jab burro; burro won't kick javelina; javelina won't drink water; water won't quench fire; fire won't burn stick; stick won't poke collie; collie won't herd steer; steer won't go in corral; and I won't get home for chili."

The cowhand said, "See that pretty gal over yonder? If she'll give me a kiss, I'll chase the armadillo."

Zeke sided up to the pretty gal. With a tip of his hat he said, "Gal, gal, kiss the cowhand. Cowhand won't chase armadillo; armadillo won't dig cactus; cactus won't jab burro; burro won't kick javelina; javelina won't drink water; water won't quench fire; fire won't burn stick; stick won't poke collie; collie won't herd steer; steer won't go in corral; and I won't get home for chili."

But the pretty gal wouldn't kiss the cowhand unless a mockingbird sang her a song.

Zeke looked up and saw a mocking-bird perched in a cottonwood tree. He tipped his hat and said, "Mockingbird, mockingbird, sing the gal a song. Gal won't kiss cowhand; cowhand won't chase armadillo; armadillo won't dig cactus; cactus won't jab burro; burro won't kick javelina; javelina won't drink water; water won't quench fire; fire won't burn stick; stick won't poke collie; collie won't herd steer; steer won't go in corral; and I won't get home for chili."

But the mockingbird said, "Bring me a bluebonnet flower, and I'll sing the pretty gal a song."

Zeke fetched a bluebonnet, gave it to the mockingbird, and galloped back to the longhorn.

The mockingbird sang the pretty gal a song; the pretty gal kissed the cowhand.

The cowhand chased the armadillo;

the armadillo dug the cactus;

the cactus jabbed the burro;

the burro kicked the javelina;

the javelina drank the water.

The water quenched the fire;

the fire burned the stick;

the stick poked the collie;

the collie herded the steer.

The steer ran into the corral . . .

. . . and Zeke got home for a big bowl of chili.
The chili was so hot, Zeke ran to the well to get a long, tall drink of water.

He tipped his hat and said, "Bucket, bucket, draw me a drink."

But the bucket wouldn't draw him a drink.

Zeke threw his hat on the ground, sat down on the porch, and shouted, "Doggone it, not again!"

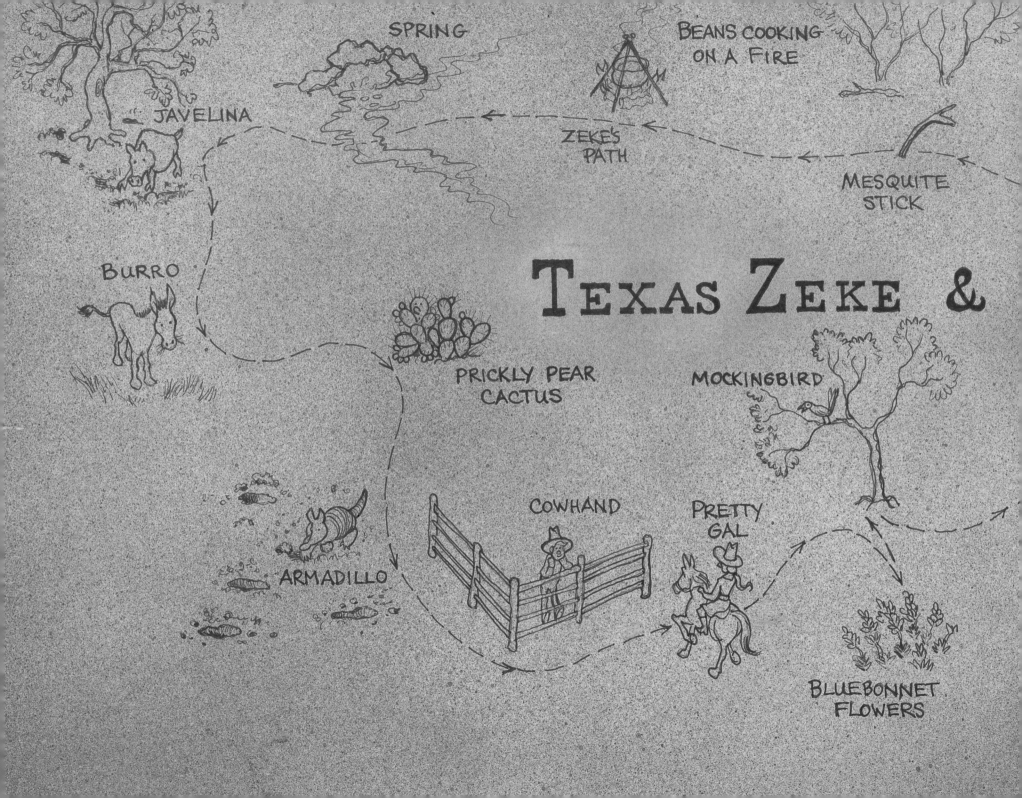